Looking
for the Song

Happy 1 Birthday
Caleb + Grant
Love Grandma +
Grandpa

A Fable of
Spiritual Journeying

Blessings, Roberta!
Love, Joan

By Joan Saalfeld, SNJM

Illustrations by
Mary Bertoli, SNJM

ISBN 0-9764223-0-1

Printed in U.S.A.

First printing, December 2004

The text type was set in Adobe Caslon and Engaged.
The display type was set in Kelt.
Mary Bertoli's illustrations were originally rendered in paper collage.
Book design by Anna Lageson-Kerns, Anna Banana Designs.

For all seekers

of the Song

The stars would come rushing down to her in a tremendous shining river of light, encircling her, holding
her close, making her feel like one of them. Best of all,
when they came, she heard the wonderful Song.

Nosrep Pronunciation Guide

Yadyreve	*Yah* di reev
Nosrep	*Nahs* rep
Reza	*Ree* zah
Draykcab	*Dray* cab
Laer	*Lay* air
Yranidro	Ee *rahn* i droe
Erac	*Eh* rack
Netsil	*Net* sil
Erawa	Eh *rah* wah
Ekaw	*Eh* kah
Nepo	*Nee* poe
Azer	*Ay* zer

Chapter One

Not long ago, in a land not far away, a small figure hurried out into the spring night. The land, which is not unlike our own, is called Yadyreve, and the people, who are not unlike ourselves, are called Nosreps. On this night, this Nosrep girl passed under her blossoming apple tree, and lay down in the grass behind her house. She was of good heart and deep spirit, and her name was Reza.

Reza brushed a black curl out of her eyes and waited. She usually enjoyed feeling the cool, prickly green on her arms and legs, and she usually loved listening to the quiet dark — seeing the stars so far away, gentle and beautiful. For when she was quite small she had discovered that she could look and look at the stars until she didn't know who she was or where she was. The stars would come rushing down to her in a tremendous shining river of light, encircling her, holding her close, making her feel like one of them. Best of all, when they came, she heard the wonderful Song.

The Song was astonishing and golden and haunting, bigger than the stars. *Big.* Full of tenderness, laughter, beauty and knowing. Completely comfortable and completely new. It seemed to be singing from inside and outside Reza at the same time. It filled her up and became part of herself for a whole day or more, making her want to sing all the time. The Song made her feel as if she were shining and beautiful and important. It made her love everybody and everything. She knew that as long as she could hear that Song, nothing could ever hurt her and she would never be afraid.

But now Reza was afraid. For many nights she had been coming out to look and look at the stars and to hear the Song, but only darkness and silence surrounded her. She waited. She hoped. She cried out to the stars, but they did not come. She drained her eyes with looking, but no star showed itself. They had gone away and they had taken the Song with them.

Reza lay as she always did, but now she hated the prickles and the coolness. Everything seemed against her, making her lost and lonely here in her own backyard! She jumped up and brushed herself off, going inside her cottage to get away from the dark that had been so friendly before. But it did not help to light a lamp or huddle in her bed. She had done that every night. The dark was everywhere, even in the lamplight. Even in the daytime. It wasn't friendly. Just dark. Inside and outside. Layer upon layer of darkness. *Dark.* Without the Song every part of her life became gloom. Everything seemed drab and uninteresting. She did not care about anything. Nothing made sense.

At first she had gone into Draykcab, the nearby village, to get help. She found it hard to talk about what had happened, and often cried when she tried to tell other Nosreps about it. And as soon as she started to cry, they seemed to think she was lonely or sick or sad in some ordinary way.

"There, there, Reza," one or the other would say. "You'll get over it."

When she told them about the Song, they looked at her as if she were not-at-all-right in her mind, and suggested she take medicine or find a nicer cottage to live in. But in her young life Reza had been lonely and sick and sad in ordinary ways, and she knew this was different. She also knew, though she did not know how to say it, that the Song gave her energy and made her more herself. It made her free and unafraid and able to do things she couldn't otherwise do.

Suddenly Reza sat up. What if the stars hadn't left and taken the Song? What if the Song had gone away and the stars had followed? Her heart held its breath. What if *she* had done something to make the Song go away? Her mind sifted and strained. She couldn't think of anything, but maybe she had done something and didn't know it. Big tears rolled down her cheeks. She felt sick and cold and numb.

Reza didn't want to leave her little house and yard and apple tree, but there seemed no other

The dark was everywhere, even in the lamplight. Even in the daytime. It wasn't friendly. Just dark. Inside and outside. Layer upon layer of darkness. **Dark.**

way. If the Song no longer came to her, if the stars had followed it away... she would have to go, too. She would leave her home in the Land of Yadyreve, and go looking for the Song. And if she had done something to send it away, she would find out what it was, and... and say how sorry she was, and promise to never ever do it again. If only she could hear the Song.

Chapter Two

In the morning Reza put on the blue sweater with pockets that had been her mother's, her brown traveling trousers, and her chartreuse hat with a very blue feather. She opened the little tin of peppermints her father had left her and found that only six remained. Reza knew that her father himself had traveled long distances on the strength of a single peppermint, and she was glad she had not yet eaten them all. She placed the peppermints in her left sweater pocket and a clean handkerchief in her right. She said good-bye to her little house and backyard and apple tree, and set out.

Her short legs did not take her very far very fast, but because she had never been away from Yadyreve before, everything looked new, and by noon she felt that she had traveled a long way from home. By mid afternoon she came to a river that shimmered and gleamed almost like her river of stars. She sat down beside it and looked and looked. It sang a Song of movement and mystery, but it wasn't *the* Song.

"Want to talk?" said a big voice behind her.

Reza turned around to see a not-at-all-short Nosrep, rubbing his hands together and looking at her with very blue eyes. Yes, the exact same blue as the feather in her hat.

"Talk?" she asked, somewhat bewildered by the enormous black shoes sticking out from under the fellow's robe.

"My name's Erac, he boomed. "And I live here by the River Laer." He sat down beside her. "You look so glum. Sometimes talking helps."

Reza stared at the dust on the hem of his rough, white garment. She was wondering how to ask for directions when she didn't know where she was going. She opened her mouth, but all she could do was repeat, "Glum?"

She said goodbye to her little house and backyard and apple tree, and set out.

"You know," he thundered, "glum!" His voice and shoulders and mouth all fell downward. Even the white hair around his ears suddenly lay limp. "Blue, sad, down-in-the-mouth." Then he straightened up and asked earnestly, "Do you speak Nosrep?"

Reza giggled.

He let out a great guffaw. "That's better!" he said.

"Yes, I do speak Nosrep," Reza said. "I just don't know what to say."

"Are you lost?" he asked in a kind, but not-at-all-quiet tone.

"No, I'm... er..."

"Are you looking for something?" As Reza nodded, he rubbed his hands together as if he'd suspected it all along. "By the by, where'd you get the feather?"

Reza's hand felt the feather in her hat as she said, "I found it in my backyard. I never saw the bird who left it, but if the rest is like this feather, it must be a very pretty bird."

"That what you're looking for?"

"What?"

"The bird that left the feather... That what you're looking for?"

"No... no, it's a Song... a beautiful Song."

"Did it come with the feather?"

Reza's black eyes widened. "No," she said carefully, "it came with... with stars..."

"Oh, stars!" he boomed. "Stars are good, too." He thought a moment. "A bit dramatic, but good!"

"You mean you know about the Song?"

He nodded.

"And I'm not crazy or bad for wanting to find it?"

"Oh, no. That would be exactly the wrong idea. Lots of Nosreps are looking."

"Really?"

"Oh, yes." His voice bristled with vitality and his eyes got bluer. The short white hair around his ears seemed to crackle with electricity. "It's not unusual to go looking. Some just don't know what they're looking for."

Reza could hardly believe her ears. She had found someone who knew what she was talking about! She found herself telling Erac everything, even the part about possibly doing something wrong that had made the Song go away.

"Oh, no," he boomed. "That would be another exactly wrong idea." Then, for the first time, he spoke quietly. "You didn't do anything wrong, Reza. The darkness just comes."

Reza was so relieved she felt a knot in her throat and a drip forming in her left eye. But before a good weep could get going, Erac roared like a big ocean wave, "Well, time to go!"

"Go where?" Reza sniffed.

"Have to cross the River Laer. No getting around it. Bridge up the way here. I'll show you." With that, he stood up and up, and offered Reza his hand. As they walked along the river together, she could feel the life coursing through Erac's fingers. In his touch she felt the same life that she now saw in the river, and that she had always felt when she heard the Song.

Very soon they came to a tiny bridge of cunning design and multiple colors. "Good-bye," Erac boomed, and helped her step onto the bridge. "Go to Yranidro. Take care. I'll be thinking of yoooooou!" His big voice faded as the river stood still and the bridge began to flow. She held her breath until Erac became a white speck calling, "Ta!" Then the bridge stopped, and the river began to flow again. Reza was on the other side.

Chapter Three

As Reza stepped from the bridge to the land, she heard someone humming and la-la-la-ing. A low, melodious "Mmmmmm — la, la, la, la." Walking around a stand of scraggy pine trees, Reza saw a Nosrep woman in a long sleeved brown dress on her hands and knees, digging in what looked to be a vegetable garden. Every time she stuck her trowel into the earth, she stopped humming, and let out a small, "Uh." When she saw Reza she said, "Oh, good. Someone to help me up." She stretched out her not-at-all-clean hands to Reza.

"Of course," said Reza, stepping right up to help. After some experimenting, it became clear that she was too short to pull the woman up by the hand. So Reza lodged herself under a brown armpit, and the woman braced one hand on Reza's head. Slowly she rose up and stood swaying.

"Thank you," she said, letting go of Reza. "Been there since the start of spring. Fell down. Couldn't get up." She brushed herself off. "My name's Netsil." She looked keenly at Reza and cocked her head. "What's yours?"

Reza said her name and then, "Here? Since the start of spring?"

Netsil uttered a low, beautiful laugh. "Yes," she said. "I slipped in the rain. Bad knees. No way to get back up. So I stopped trying and began to listen." She looked down at the lush little garden. "Soon I began to hear the beans and peas choking, so I helped them by clearing the weeds. I've been tending them ever since. The others, too. And they've been giving me good things to eat." She showed her basket half filled with peas and beans, beet greens and strawberries, rhubarb and lettuce, and other things Reza didn't recognize. "Very glad you came along. Want something to eat?"

They went into Netsil's house. After they had enjoyed a tasty vegetable dish, Netsil turned to

Reza, offered her a big strawberry, and said, "So how *are* you?"

Something in Netsil's completely attentive face made Reza not say "Fine," as she often did with Nosreps who asked, but who didn't really want to know. She found herself telling Netsil exactly how she was. Sick, numb, unhappy. Looking for the Song.

Netsil didn't tell Reza to see a doctor, or that she'd outgrow the need for the Song. She just listened with her whole attention, her brown eyes reflecting Reza's sadness. "Um-mmmm," Netsil said, in a warm and comforting way.

And Reza knew that Netsil had really heard and understood.

"You know," Netsil said after a minute or two of silence, "you might have to learn to look and listen in a different way from the one you're used to."

Reza got very quiet. She shivered and said, "But the dark…"

"The dark… is only the dark," Netsil said very quietly. She paused, and then went on, "It's like silence."

Reza didn't say anything, but she wanted to remind Netsil that silence was exactly the problem. The Song and the stars had gone away, and she was left with darkness and silence!

Netsil went on, "Silence can help, you know. But you have to listen to it. It can help you find the Between."

"Between?"

Netsil nodded toward the raggy little pine tree outside her house. "Look at its branches," she said. "Not just the shapes made by the branches and needles, but look at the spaces in between."

Reza stared at the little tree.

"The Between lets you see the shape. No spaces, no pine tree."

Reza stared at the Between. She didn't know if she liked this Between thing, but something about it did ring true. Could it have something to do with why the Song had gone away? It struck her that she never thought so much, or cared so much, about the Song until after she no longer heard it.

"Most do not look closely enough at the spaces," Netsil's melodic voice flowed on. "And most do not listen carefully enough to the silence. If you do, perhaps you will hear the Song again in new ways."

"If only I could," Reza said. "If only I could hear the Song again."

Then Netsil told her of a land farther on, where Nosreps went to learn to see the spaces and hear the silences. "It's called Yranidro," she said.

"That's where Erac told me to go," Reza breathed. "Oh, tell me how to get there!"

Chapter Four

So the next morning Netsil took Reza to the edge of the woods and showed her the path to follow to Yranidro, and Reza eagerly set out. As she came to the first bend, she turned to wave to Netsil, who called, "Stay on the path, even if it's long. Listen to the silence. Look for the Between."

"Will it be long?" Reza wondered to herself. Neither Erac nor Netsil had said. This question faded, however, as she entered the very dense woods. Tall trees and undergrowth made a tangle of green and brown. In the beginning, Reza tried to look at the Between of the trees, but that seemed to take too long and she didn't think she was getting anywhere. She just wanted to find Yranidro. That should be soon enough to pay attention to looking and listening.

The farther Reza walked, the denser and darker the forest became. She did not want to go deeper into the woods, but she did so want to hear the Song again. So she pulled her sweater close around her, enjoyed a peppermint, and hurried on her journey.

Suddenly the path took a sharp turn and ended with the trees opening onto a lush meadow. A stone's throw into the meadow Reza could see a still figure standing among the grasses and wild-flowers. As she approached, Reza realized that it was a bird — a not-at-all-short, not-at-all-wide heron bird. Slowly it lifted a stick-like leg and held it in the air before putting it down again a few inches from where it started. Then the other bony leg went up, poised, and slowly lowered. The heron swung its big, pointed beak in Reza's direction. It raised its eyebrows and blinked its eyes and said in a croaky voice, "Where are you going?"

Reza was so startled by the heron speaking that she took a step backward. "I'm... I'm..." She looked at his beak. "I'm going to Yranidro," she said quickly, glad she now knew the name of her destination.

He leaned down and put one of his yellow eyes very close to her face, once again raising his eyebrows and blinking.

"Ah, Yranidro. And what will you do there?" He leaned down and put one of his yellow eyes very close to her face, once again raising his eyebrows and blinking.

"Well, I'm... looking for the Song," she finished in a rush.

He jumped back, flapping his big wings and croaking happily. "Are you?" he said. "Will you allow me to show you the path on the other side of the meadow? And perhaps stop with me at the spring for a drink of water?"

"I'd be very grateful," said Reza, much relieved. "Do many come this way looking?"

"Quite a few," he said. He began leading Reza in his hesitant, high-stepping way.

He was so friendly that, as she followed him, Reza said, "My name is Reza. What's yours?"

"I am Erawa." As he said his name he turned toward her, now not at all a heron, but a tall, stately Nosrep man in a flowing black robe. He still raised his eyebrows and blinked his eyes, but now his eyes were gray, and very kind. He walked ahead of her through the grassland with great dignity, cautioning her to watch her step when they came to rough ground or a rocky place.

Reza was struck dumb. She followed in amazement, wondering at the mixture of awe and familiarity she was feeling about Erawa. It reminded her of the Song.

They sat beside the spring and had a refreshing drink. He pointed out to her every creature, every flower, every blade of the meadow — every bird song and insect hum. She caught her breath at how intimately he knew them. They all seemed part of himself. She wished she could know them so well. At last he led her to a footpath and said, "This path will take you to Yranidro, Reza."

When he said her name, Reza began to cry. "I don't know why tears are coming," she said. "I should be happy."

"I know why," he said, kindly. "You want the Song very much. It means everything to you."

At this Reza cried harder. "Maybe I want it too much," she sobbed, taking the handkerchief from her sweater pocket.

"You can't want the Song too much," Erawa said. "It is worth whatever it takes." He still spoke in the croaky voice of the heron, but Reza thought she had never heard such a beautiful sound, except, of course, for the Song.

As Reza took to the path, Erawa called after her, "Watch for Nepo when you come out of the forest. She will help you cross the va-a-ast Eno Sea, but until then, stay on the path and go deeper into the woods." Then he turned and began his stately walk back into that abandoned, grassy place, lifting a stick-like foot and shaking enormous wings.

Chapter Five

The path that had begun so broadly at the meadow quickly now became not-at-all broad — so narrow, in fact, that Reza had to turn sideways to squeeze through some places. It got darker and Reza began to slow her pace. She couldn't see very far down the path and she would have been quite frightened if, in her mind's ear, she could not still hear Erawa's croaky voice telling her, "It is worth whatever it takes." It was dark, though. She couldn't help imagining strange creatures looking out at her from the tangled roots and low slung branches. And she couldn't help wondering what it would take.

Some of the branches had thorns on them and caught at her sweater as she passed. Cold and tired, Reza began to feel anxious about what would happen to her after all. Finally she could see that the path narrowed down to a small opening about the size of her fist. Reza groaned. She could never get through that.

Reza stepped back and sat down on a low stone. She took a peppermint from her pocket and put it in her mouth. She remembered how her father used to smack his lips when the pungent sweetness touched his tongue. It made her smile, and she smacked her own lips as she looked around. She did not feel quite as tired.

A miniscule bit of light came through the opening. It might lead her to the end of the woods if she could just find a way through. She remembered Netsil and decided to try to listen to the silence and look at the Between.

Reza stared at the tiny opening and became as still as the stone she was sitting on. She sat and sat. She did not know how long; it seemed a very long time and no time at all. She did not hear the Song, but after a while she did not know who she was or where she was. When she came to herself, she decided to try to squeeze through the opening, even though it seemed impossible. She pressed her forehead against the tiny circle of light and pushed hard until suddenly, to her surprise, she was out of the woods and sitting on a sunny cliff, overlooking the broad, blue-green Eno Sea.

Before Reza could think how she got there, a rhythmic booming consumed her attention. Below, huge waves picked up loads of loose rocks and pounded them down on the shore like a big heartbeat. She sat transfixed by the boom and splash each time a wave slammed down another load. It reverberated through her whole body.

A boat sailing by in the offing seemed to be headed in Reza's direction. When it got closer, she could see a not-at-all-tall Nosrep woman at the helm, one hand shading her eyes, the other steering the boat. A jaunty little captain's hat sat on her head of silver hair. A whole row of Nosreps stared at Reza from the deck as three more worked to drop the anchor.

"Waiting for me?" the small captain called up to Reza.

Reva tried to make herself heard over the work of the waves. "Are you Nepo?"

The captain nodded and called, "Come aboard."

Reza didn't see how she was going to do that since the boat was so far off, and the cliff so high, and the waves so big! But she did want to go to Yranidro.

"Please help me!" she called.

At that, one of the Nosreps on deck threw a tiny, multi-colored rubber raft overboard, and it floated toward the cliff. "Get in," Nepo called.

Reza looked at the bright speck bobbing in the surf.

"I can't do that!" she cried. "I can't launch out on the ocean in that little bitty thing! And it's too far away. How would I ever get to it?"

"Have to, if you want to come," Nepo called. "Can't bring the ship any closer." She looked around at the other Nosreps. They were all sizes and ages and shapes. "All together…" she said.

And all together they yelled up at Reza, "Jump!"

Reza shrank back. Who were these Nosreps telling her to jump! Had they lost their not-at-all-right minds? She grabbed hold of the only bush on the ledge and hung on.

"What is your name?" called Nepo.

"Reza," she shouted as a big wave slammed down its load of rocks. She tightened her hold on the bush.

"Reza, come," called Nepo.

Reza knew she could not, would not, jump. Nothing could be so dangerous and stupid and … but Nepo's voice calling her name floated above all other sounds, echoing inside her, loosening her fingers. "Come, Reza…"

She found herself letting go and sliding over the ledge. She held onto her hat and plunged deep into the water. Down, down she went. As she passed a big spotted fish, he examined the feather on her hat with a shiny, black eye, not unlike her own. He waved a feathery fin as she floated to the surface right next to the raft.

The Nosreps on the boat cheered.

"Climb into the raft," cried one from the crow's nest.

"You can do it," another called from the boat's railing.

Reza flopped into the bobbing raft and shut her eyes. At first she couldn't do anything but hang on. Then, frightened and excited, she felt the ocean's enormous life coursing under the rubber skin of the raft. It reminded her of Erac's hand, and she relaxed a bit. As she rode the raft, the waves seemed both still and moving, as if she were sitting on the pulse of the wide world, all the while holding her breath.

When the raft started to drift away from the ship, Nepo called, "Pick up the paddle, Reza!"

A boat sailing by in the offing... headed in Reza's direction...

"REZA, REZA, REZA!" Everyone on the boat was calling now.

Reza let go her hold on the side of the raft, picked up the paddle, and started to dig into the water to guide the raft toward the ship. When she got close enough, the Nosreps threw her a line and hauled her aboard, raft and all. Suddenly she found herself in the same boat with others on the way to Yranidro. Gratefully, she shook their offered hands and looked into their friendly faces.

That night Nepo found Reza on deck gazing up. "Ah, the stars," Nepo said. "They are clear and beautiful tonight." Then Nepo saw Reza's tears. She was just Reza's size, though a good deal older, and they looked at each other eye to eye. "Are stars so important?" Nepo asked.

So Reza told her all. The stars. The Song. All of it. "I haven't seen them for so long," she said. "Now I see them, but they stay far away… and I don't hear the Song. It's almost worse than not seeing them at all!"

"Ah," Nepo said. "The Song was a gift. It made you go looking because you *know* there is more." She spoke even more kindly. "But such a gift makes it hard to let go when it's time."

"Let go?" Reza thought of the cliff and the waves and shuddered.

"You must hold such a gift lightly, and let it go when it's time."

Reza cried silently for some moments. Then in a very small voice she asked, "Is it time?"

"Yes," Nepo said gently.

So they sailed a long while on the vast Eno Sea, and each day Reza felt her old way of looking at things changing more. She began to accept whatever was before her, and not to want more or less. Nepo and Reza and the others sat together on the deck each day, looking at the empty sky and endless sea, listening to the great pulsing world beneath the surface. They listened and listened until all were clear-eyed and open, ready for Yranidro.

Chapter Six

When they finally sailed into Yranidro harbor, Reza was somehow not surprised at how small and familiar, how ordinary it looked. When she had first heard of Yranidro, she had expected something special, something exciting. But now, after sitting and listening to the sea of life with Nepo and the others, the humbleness of the little town seemed quite natural and fitting. On the dock a sign said "WELCOME YRANIDRO NOSREP," and a little song sparrow was sitting on it, singing with its whole tiny being. Reza raised her eyebrows and blinked her eyes and suddenly saw that she had been reading part of the sign backwards. It really said "WELCOME ORDINARY PERSON."

Other names now came clear to her — Erac, Netsil, Erawa! She laughed aloud.

And it came to her how good it was to be in this ordinary place by the Eno Sea. No one told her, but it seemed quite clear that the ordinary water she heard lapping here and now, also washed some unseen, timeless shore. And the song of the sparrow tweedling on the signpost was somehow connected to the Song — that Song of otherness, and mystery, and life that had come to her with the stars.

Reza settled happily into Yranidro. The days went by quickly as she learned to take delight in the beauty and goodness of ordinary things, listening to the song of each creature. But as the seasons passed, she began to feel she had learned all she could here. She began to long for her own little house, her backyard, her apple tree.

And so, one evening when she heard that Nepo was in port, Reza went to see her, and asked Nepo to show her the way back to her home. Reza thought they would wait until morning and then go to the harbor, but Nepo stretched her short legs at once and said, "Come with me." It was almost as if she had known Reza would ask — as if she had been waiting for her to ask. They walked all the way to the other edge of Yranidro, the one opposite the harbor. There an expanse of desert badlands lay before them.

Reza looked out on the desolate landscape. "You can't mean it," she said, thinking of the comfort of Nepo's rocking ship and the little community of fellow travelers on the boat.

"It is part of the way," Nepo said. "Can't go back. Have to go forward to get home." She looked at Reza earnestly — bright eye to bright eye — and Reza knew she would have to go on.

She sighed. Well, since that was the case, she would waste no time. Quickly she hugged Nepo, and the little captain's hat fell off. While Nepo was picking it up, Reza secured the feather in her own hat and set off. When she looked back, Nepo was solemnly waving, cap in hand, the light of the rising moon striking her beautiful silver hair.

"Good-bye!" called Reza. A single peppermint remained in her left sweater pocket for when she really needed it. Reza had a feeling that would be soon.

Chapter Seven

At first, the barren landscape was not so frightening as it was uncomfortable and boring. By day, empty, dry and tedious; by night, cold and unfriendly. No way to tell for sure if she was going in the right direction. No one to ask. It made Reza wonder if she really wanted to go on. Nothing interesting or satisfying or exciting was happening — only the same endless emptiness. Now that she had accepted not hearing the Song in the old way — the star way — she wanted to be places where she could hear it in the songs of things around her. Here, there didn't seem much chance of that. She fingered the peppermint in her pocket and kept walking.

At length she saw what looked like a dead tree in the distance. Since nothing else broke the skyline, Reza headed toward it. When she got nearer, she could see a bird — a hawk — perched on a limb, a big rock right below. The hawk's eyes were closed and it seemed asleep or dead.

She was deciding whether to stop a bit or just go on when the thing opened its eyes half-mast and its beak full blast, letting out an ear-piercing shriek and ruffling its brown and gold feathers.

It startled Reza so that she fell down on the rocky ground and covered her head with her hands.

"What is the matter?" the hawk asked in a cultured voice.

Reza looked at it through her fingers. "Why did you scream like that?" she whispered.

The hawk made a movement with his wings that was close to a shrug. "I like it," he said. "It is my nature."

"But you scared me. And there was no need…"

"Some things are frightening. I appear to be one of them." He seemed to enjoy the idea. "Not much entertainment out here."

"But…"

"Just be frightened and go on."

"But how can I go on in this awful place?"

At the question, the hawk's yellow eyes opened wide, and so did his wings. "You can go on as the great world itself goes on — moment by moment by moment!" He gave another towering shriek and loosened his talons from the branch.

Reza shut her eyes tight against the mind-bending sound, and when she opened them, a Nosrep man in a brown and gold robe was sitting on the rock.

This bird-to-man transformation was starting to seem familiar. "Do you know a heron named Erawa?" she asked.

He nodded. "He's my brother — my meadow brother. My name's Ekaw."

"I'm Reza," she said. She repeated his name and shook her head. "Ekaw, you certainly didn't look awake," she said.

"And you, Reza, certainly did not want to hear my song," he said.

"Song? That was no song! That was a…"

"That was my song," he said firmly.

"Ah," she said. "Ah…" She sat down. She began to understand.

Slowly, slowly, she quieted and began to listen to the badlands. After a time she heard the tiny scrape of the scorpion under the rock, the click of the beetle as it bored into the sand, the breath of the tiniest spider as it pursued the tiniest fly. And, when she no longer knew who she was or where she was, she heard the great resonating tone of the emptiness itself.

"Ah," she said again at last. "Even here."

"Especially here," said Ekaw.

...*the thing opened its eyes half-mast and its beak full blast, letting out an ear piercing shriek and ruffling its brown and gold feathers...*

"Yes," she said. "Especially here." And now she knew that the Song was not only lovely and attractive and pleasant, but scary and tedious and painful as well. Beauty and peace were not requirements — only reality.

The next morning she was surprised when she noticed a mountain — a big, red mountain — not far off. She wondered why she had not seen it before and she asked as much of Ekaw, who was sitting in the tree again.

"What difference does it make?" he said in carefully modulated tones, his eyes at half-mast. "It's there now."

"I don't understand why I didn't see it all the time I was walking. It's so big."

"It was there," he said, closing his eyes completely, then opening them wide and giving a little frustrated shriek. "You just were not awake."

"Oh," she said in a very small voice.

After a moment he added, "You will be able to see your homeland from the top."

"From the *top!*"

Ekaw sighed. "Always the repetition," he said to himself, shutting his eyes completely again.

"I'm sorry," Reza said quickly. "I understand. Thank you."

"You're welcome," he said. Reza thought she saw his hooked beak soften into a little smile.

Chapter Eight

started out for the red mountain, toying with the last peppermint in her pocket. When she got to the mountain's foot and saw the path zig-zagging across its face, she did not even hesitate. She began the climb at once.

The sun was shining brightly and the sky was very blue, and Reza felt happy to be going home. When she got quite high, she could see all the way to Yranidro and the Eno Sea. Even more interesting were the nearby white clouds that frisked in the wind, swirling around the mountain's very red edge. Reza stopped and watched the clouds move and dive until she didn't know who she was or where she was. And when she began to know again, the sun had started to go down on the other side of the mountain.

In the twilight Reza decided to start climbing again. There was still time before it would be too dark to see. Coming to the next switchback, she was startled by the sound of moaning from somewhere off the path. When she followed the sounds, she found a Nosrep child weeping, his face twisted in pain, his whole body shivering with cold.

Reza immediately threw off her sweater and put it over him. She unwrapped her last peppermint and held it to his lips. The boy's eyes opened and his tongue licked the candy lightly before taking it into his mouth. He began to revive a little and said between sobs, "Don't leave me."

Reza took the little boy in her arms. "I won't leave you," she said. "What's your name?"

"I don't know," he said simply. "They called me 'Boy' when they wanted me, and they left me when I couldn't keep up."

Reza didn't leave him. As she held him through the cold night, warming him with her own body and reassuring him whenever he woke, she thought of her house and yard and apple tree. She began to fear that she would never see them again.

Chapter Nine

The sun was most welcome in the morning, bringing its brightness and warmth. Reza and the little boy sat up and became very still as they watched life awaken across the plain below. At another time, Reza might have stared in wonder until she didn't know who she was or where she was, but now she attended to the child instead.

Reza could see that they were about two-thirds of the way up the mountain and she asked the child if he could walk. He tried repeatedly, but fell each time, too weak to do more than sit up. She felt both pockets of the blue sweater, now wrapped around the boy, but there were no more peppermints. So Reza gathered him in her arms and stood up. She didn't know how long she could struggle up the red path, but she knew she could not leave him, even to go for help.

Reza managed to carry the boy through the day, but the path was very steep, and she had to stop often. In the twilight, she sank down, unable to go on. "I won't leave you," she said to the sleeping boy. She held him to herself, against the mountain's chill, and fell asleep.

For the next two days Reza tried to reach the top of the mountain, her body aching with the weight of the child. But the way seemed endless, the task impossible.

During the third night, the darkness began to rumble. Reza woke and saw slashes of lightning advancing across the valley, as thunder clattered overhead. Sparse raindrops became a downpour, soaking Reza and the boy and making small rivers all around them. Now Reza did not even think of her safe home or yard or apple tree. Aware only of the storm, extravagant and wild, she held on. She embraced the boy, and the storm, as best she could.

When the bright sunlight touched her face, Reza was dreaming that someone was calling her. Then, as she sat up straight, she realized it wasn't a dream!

"Yoo-hoo," sang a big familiar voice. "Anyone there?"

"Erac!" she breathed. Then she shouted, "Erac!"

Erac came bounding down the steep path, his big shoes and white robe covered with red-mountain dust, a large bag swinging at his side. "There you are!" he said. "How about some breakfast?"

To Reza's utter amazement, he opened his bag and set out bowls and spoons and dry cereal, raspberries and a flask of fresh milk. "Oatie Floaties," he boomed. "My favorite." He rubbed his hands together.

"Oh, Erac," Reza said, filling a bowl and handing it to the boy. "We're so glad to see you." As the little fellow began scooping spoonfuls of cereal into his mouth, Reza took Erac's big hand in both of hers and held it to her cheek. "Thank you," she breathed.

"I got worried and came looking. Who's this?" Erac asked, sprinkling raspberries on the child's cereal with his free hand.

"He doesn't have a name. He was alone and very weak when I found him. I couldn't leave him, even to go look for help."

Erac pierced her with his very blue eyes. The white hair around his ears bristled and snapped. "Of course not!" he bellowed. "It would be leaving yourself!"

"Yoursel-l-l-l-f…" echoed down the mountain, making Reza blink.

"Yes," she said with wonder. "It would be…" She knew then that the child's song of pain was somehow her song, too.

"We'll name him Azer," Erac thundered. "His name is Azer!"

Reza laughed in delight, and the child stopped eating and laughed, too. Erac's great "Ha, ha, ha!" reverberated through the morning and into the clouds and out into the very blue sky. They ate their

Erac came bounding down the steep path, his big shoes and white robe covered with red-mountain dust, a large bag swinging at his side.

Oatie Floaties laughing, and the raspberries sparkled in the sun like jewels.

When breakfast was over, Erac picked up the boy and took Reza by the hand. It was not at all long before they made it to the top, and they sat for a while looking at what lay before them on the other side — the meadow, the forest, the River Laer — and beyond the river, Reza's homeland and village. Reza smiled and wondered how Azer would like her house and backyard and apple tree.

Swinging down the mountain with Erac was easy, and soon they approached the meadow. Azer rode on Erac's shoulder, pointing in delight at goldfinches flitting and twittering among the thistles and wildflowers. As the three of them stood amid the teeming peace of the place, a shadow passed over them. They looked up and Reza caught her breath as a bird with not-at-all-narrow wings circled above them.

"Erawa!" she called.

The heron floated down in front of them and bowed deeply to each in turn. To Reza he croaked, "I'm so glad to see you!" When he inclined his head toward her he still had a heron's beak, but when he stood up straight and faced her, it was the stately Nosrep who raised his eyebrows and blinked his eyes. "Was it worth it?" he whispered.

"Oh, yes," Reza breathed. "It's worth whatever it takes." She told him all that it did take, about Nepo, and about his brother, Ekaw, and finally about finding Azer on the mountain and not being able to leave him.

At this last, Erawa said, "So, the face of the other becomes your own face." Reza nodded solemnly, and Erac rubbed his hands together, smiling.

They rested and refreshed themselves while Erawa croaked and flapped happily around them. He made them laugh by singing his fractured heron songs, and he took Azer for short flights around the meadow on his back. At last they left him in late afternoon. Reza's last look found the heron with one bony foot raised as if to take a not-at-all-insignificant step.

Just before nightfall, they came to the end of the woods when they heard a soft, melodious "Mmmmmmm — la, la, la."

They hurried around the last turn and there, in front of them, was a brown-clothed Nosrep woman sitting on the forest floor putting mushrooms in her basket. "Netsil!" Reza cried, rushing to her. "Oh, Netsil, did you fall again?"

"Oh, no," said Netsil smiling. "I thought you'd be coming soon and I wanted mushrooms for our stew."

Erac bowed and helped her up. "Stew!" he boomed, beaming. "What a good idea!"

"All of you are most welcome," Netsil said, touching Azer on the cheek. "Who is this fine fellow?"

As they walked along together, Reza told Netsil all that had happened to her, and how she had found Azer, and how Erac had found them.

"And did you ever find the Song?" asked Netsil.

Reza took a breath and replied that she had learned that every creature has its very own song, which, at the same time, is part of the big wonderful Song. "So now I try to listen to every song — even the song of the hawk, and the silence, and the dark — even the song of pain or need."

"And?" said Netsil.

"And somehow it is all *my* Song."

"Yes," said Netsil. "One Song."

Chapter Ten

Erac, and Azer stayed the night at Netsil's house and began the last part of their trip early the next morning. When they reached the River Laer, they decided that before traveling to the bridge, they would eat the lunch Netsil had packed for them. Reza handed around the sandwiches. Azer began to eat immediately, but Erac looked away. He kept clearing his throat over and over.

"H'rumph, h'rumph!" he said loudly.

"What is it, Erac?" asked Reza.

"You must go on to your home, and I must stay here at the River Laer."

"Yes?" she said.

"Azer could help me in my work here, and carry it on when I'm gone. I would teach him about the river and the bridge, and…"

Azer was sitting on Erac's shoulder hanging on to the tuft of white hair over Erac's right ear. When he heard Erac's words, he stopped eating and said in wonder, "You mean you want me? You want me to stay here at the river with you?"

"Yes," boomed Erac. "That would be exactly the right idea."

Azer waved his sandwich and pulled Erac's hair. He opened his mouth and no words came. But Reza saw his silent song of joy.

Reza gazed at the River Laer flashing past them, bubbling and splashing and singing its song. She had assumed that Azer would go home with her, and, almost without knowing it, she had been making plans for his life with her. But the light in his face now was the very same as that in Erac's face, the very same brightness and dazzle as that of the River Laer. In a blink she knew Azer would

...they walked to the colorful flowing bridge and crossed the River Laer. Then, with promises of future visits on both sides, Reza gave her blue feather to Azer as a parting gift...

stay with Erac. He should stay and sing his song here with Erac and the river. And she thought of Erac, too. Erac, who took care of everyone, would have someone to care for him when his day of need came.

So after lunch the three walked to the colorful flowing bridge and crossed the River Laer. Then, with promises of future visits on both sides, Reza gave her blue feather to Azer as a parting gift, kissed him and Erac good-bye, and set out for home.

As she got closer, the neighborhood began to look the same, and yet quite different to her. And when she came to the sign outside her village, she laughed out loud. She knew it had always said, "Welcome to the Village of Draykcab in the Land of Yadyreve." But now she could read "Welcome to the Village of Backyard in the Land of Everyday." It made her want to reach her own backyard even more.

As evening began to fall, Reza pushed through her very own gate. She found the apple tree heavy with rosy-cheeked fruit and she picked one and ate it, enjoying its crisp sweetness as never before. She lay down in the grass, which felt cool and prickly and planned how she would pick apples in the morning and take them into Draykcab and give them to Nosreps who had no apple tree. She began to think about what else she could do for those who had less than she did. They were a part of herself as surely as the last calls of the crows, or the high, pesky whine of evening mosquitoes, were part of the Song.

As it became fully dark, the stars appeared. Reza looked and looked at them, but did not beg them to come down. Instead she tried to listen to what was around her, things she hadn't noticed in her old star-gazing days. After a few moments what she heard was the familiar sound of an apple falling. "PLAWP!"

But the "aw" in the plop opened bigger and bigger and bigger until it burst into the Song

— the Song as she had never heard it before. It reached from her little yard high up to the stars and wide out to the world and beyond. A love for all that was, and all that could be, swept over her, and she did not know who or where she was.

She had come home to the Song — the Song she could now hear in her ordinary life, in her own backyard, every day.

She had come home to the Song — the Song she could now hear in her ordinary life, in her own backyard, every day.